GECKO GATHERING

by Vanessa Giancamilli

Illustrated by Kristin Kest

For Jeff, with love and thanks.— V.G.

For Harriet Kasak — you will be missed.— K²

Book copyright © 2004 Trudy Corporation

Published by Soundprints Division of Trudy Corporation, Norwalk, Connecticut.

Book design: Marcin D. Pilchowski
Book layout: Jennifer Kinon
Editor: Laura Gates Galvin
Editorial assistance: Brian E. Giblin

First Edition 2004
10 9 8 7 6 5 4 3 2 1
Printed in China

Acknowledgements:
    Our very special thanks to Kellar Autumn of Lewis & Clark College for his review and guidance.

Library of Congress Cataloging-in-Publication Data

Giancamilli, Vanessa, 1977-
    Gecko gathering / by Vanessa Giancamilli ; illustrated by Kristin Kest.--1st ed.
        p. cm. -- (Amazing animal adventures)
    Summary: A gecko spends an exciting night searching for something to eat while avoiding being eaten by some other creature.
        ISBN 1-59249-288-6 (hardcover) -- ISBN 1-59249-289-4 (micro pbk.)
        ISBN 1-59249-290-8 (pbk.)
        1. Geckos--Juvenile fiction. [1. Geckos--Fiction. 2. Rain forests--Fiction.
    3. Tibet (China)--Fiction.] I. Kest, Kristin, ill. II. Title. III. Series.

PZ10.3.G348Ge 2004
[E]--dc22
                                                                    2004002581

GECKO
GATHERING

by Vanessa Giancamilli
Illustrated by Kristin Kest

Soundprints
Where Children Discover...

It is the end of a hot day in Thailand, but Gecko's day is just beginning. As night falls and the air becomes cooler, Gecko leaves his resting spot under the petals of an orchid to begin his nightly hunt for food.

Gecko waddles quickly through the tropical forest he calls home, looking for an insect to eat. Cockroaches and moths are his favorite. In a large clearing of trees and bushes, Gecko sits still and listens for noises that will lead him to an insect. He hears a cockroach scurry into the forest.

Gecko spots the cockroach near a house in the middle of the clearing. He moves quickly toward the cockroach but hears the sound of human footsteps in the darkness.

The cockroach runs away, scared. Gecko, also frightened, begins his defensive call. "Braaak! Braaak! BRAAAK!"

The door of the house opens and the sound of the footsteps disappears. Gecko is safe, but so is the cockroach that was supposed to be his meal. Gecko moves on to find more food.

At the base of a papaya tree, Gecko finds a papaya broken open. This is a treat for Gecko! He reaches his tongue out to taste the sweet nectar. Then he reaches his tongue out to clean his eyes!

Suddenly, Gecko hears a Pangolin, a scaly animal that also lives in the tropical forest. With its snout the Pangolin is digging up grasses and mosses, looking for ants and termites to eat—and it is heading toward Gecko!

Frightened, Gecko makes a quick escape, running up the trunk of a nearby tree. He hangs upside down on one of the tree's tall branches, watching the Pangolin below as it continues on its path.

However, Gecko is not safe yet. He sees a Palm Civet crawling toward him on the branches of the tree. Gecko turns to run away, but the Palm Civet is too quick. Chomp! The Palm Civet bites off Gecko's tail! Luckily, Gecko is not hurt and, in time, a new tail will grow in.

Gecko quickly moves to safety, using his sticky toe pads to climb farther up the tree. He hears a faint sound. "Check-to, to-kay. Check-to, to-kay." It's the gathering call of other geckos. Gecko responds with his own call. "Check-to, to-kay."

Gecko sees other geckos hanging upside down from the twisted branches of the tree. He climbs past the leaves and the bright petals of the orchids growing on the tree's branches.

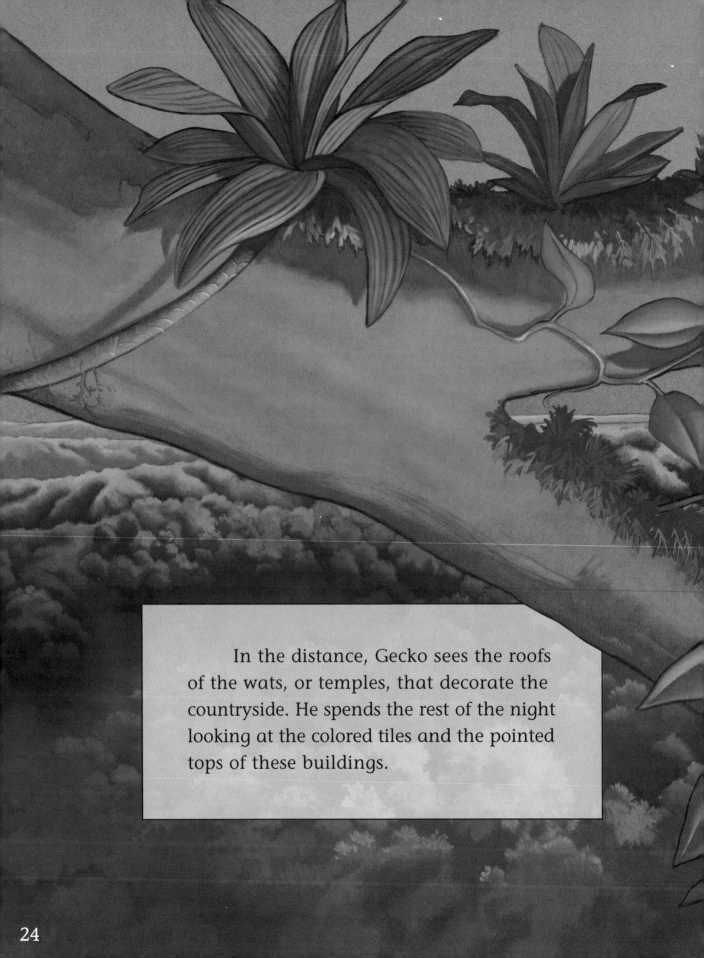

In the distance, Gecko sees the roofs of the wats, or temples, that decorate the countryside. He spends the rest of the night looking at the colored tiles and the pointed tops of these buildings.

As the sun comes up in the early morning, the temperature rises. Gecko climbs down from his perch high atop the tree. He looks for a dark place where he can hide from the bright sun. He finds a piece of tree bark that has fallen to the ground. Gecko crawls under the bark and settles in for a day of rest after a long night of adventure.

THE TOKAY GECKO LIVES IN THAILAND

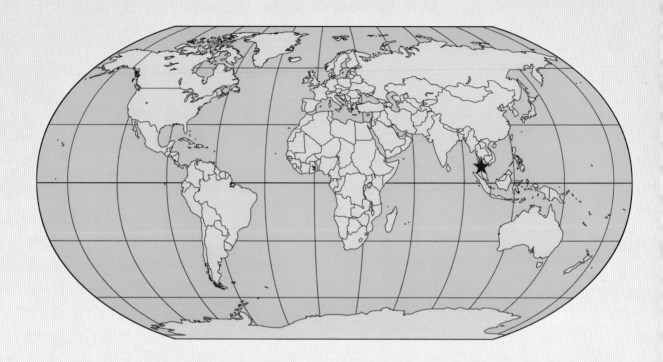

ABOUT THE TOKAY GECKO

Tokay geckos live in warm climates around the world. They can be found in sandy deserts, rocky steppes, tidal pools, tropical rain forests and mountain-top forests.

Tokay geckos have tiny hairs on the bottom of their feet that allow them to stick to almost any surface. They can even hang upside down from a piece of glass!

Tokay geckos are nocturnal, meaning they are active at night. Small insects, such as cockroaches, make up most of a gecko's diet, but geckos sometimes eat fruit nectar and flower pollen.

Tokay geckos can grow to be one foot long, though they are only three inches when they are born. They can live up to five years in captivity and have been known to live as long as twelve years in the wild.

▲ Jasmine

▲ Tokay Gecko

▲ **Arial Pitcher Plant**

▲ **Orchid**

▲ Pangolin

▲ Cockroach

PICTORIAL GLOSSARY

▲ Asian Palm Civet

▲ Golden Emporer Moth